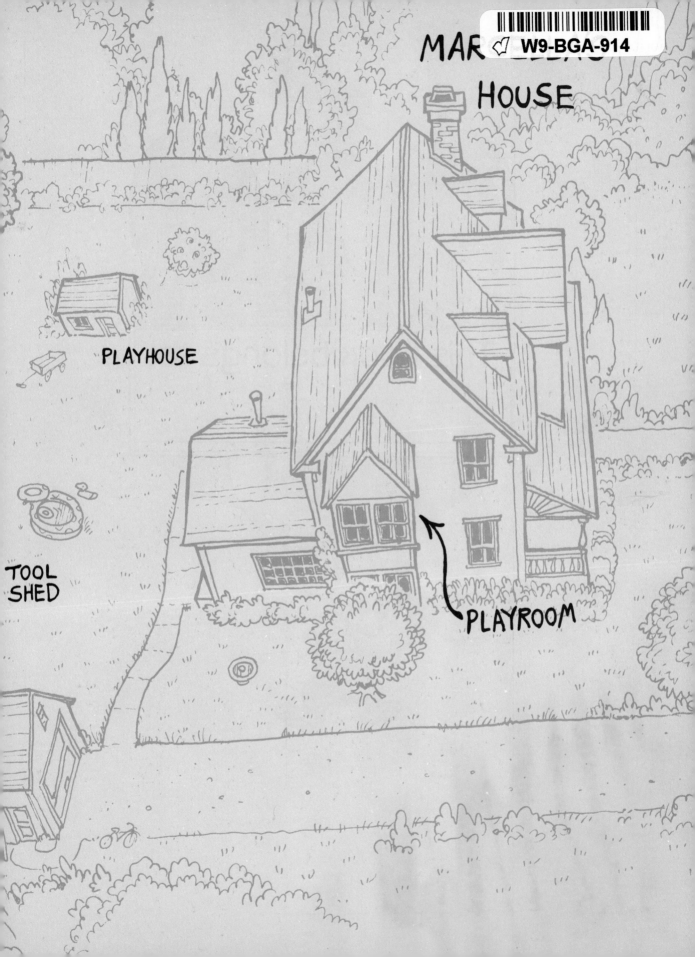

This book belongs to:

_____

Raggedy Ann & Andy's

GROUCHY BEAR'S PARADE

A LYNX BOOK

This book is published by Lynx Books, a division of Lynx Communications, Inc., 41 Madison Avenue, New York, New York 10010. The name "Lynx" together with the logotype consisting of a stylized head of a lynx is a trademark of Lynx Communications, Inc.

Raggedy Ann and Andy's Grow-and-Learn Library, the names and depictions of Raggedy Ann, Raggedy Andy and all related characters are trademarks of Macmillan, Inc.

One day in the Town Toy Store, a very cute, cuddly teddy bear woke up from his nap. The toys on the shelf near him were whispering to each other. Something was about to happen!

"What is it?" the little bear asked sleepily. "What is going on?"

A ballerina doll said, "Shhhh, a little girl is coming this way! She's going to take one of us home."

The little bear looked down the aisle. Then he sat as straight and tall as he possibly could.

Thump! The teddy bear bumped his head on the shelf.

"Ouch!" he said with a frown. That was when Marcella first saw him.

"Oh!" Marcella said to her mama. "I'd like that teddy bear. He's so cute and grouchy-looking. I'll name him Grouchy!"

"Grouchy?" he wondered. He had always been a very happy little bear. But now he wanted to please the little girl who had picked *him* out of all the dolls in the store. If she wanted him to be grouchy, that was exactly what he would be.

When Marcella got home, she took Grouchy Bear right up to the playroom and introduced him to her other dolls and toys.

"Take good care of Grouchy Bear," Marcella told Raggedy Ann as she left to go downstairs for dinner.

As soon as she was gone the dolls and toys began to talk and laugh and play a game of tag.

"Come join us, Grouchy Bear!" Raggedy Ann invited.

But Grouchy Bear wouldn't budge from his seat near the toy box.

"No, thanks," he mumbled in a grouchy voice. He was trying very hard to be as grouchy as possible.

Each day, Grouchy Bear practiced acting crankier and crankier. He wanted Marcella to be very happy she chose him in the toy store. Whenever anyone was around, he frowned. He did such a good job practicing that his playroom friends believed he really was grouchy. But most of the time, he really wasn't—not deep inside.

Then one day, The Camel with the Wrinkled Knees sneezed so hard that all of the dolls started to laugh! Grouchy Bear had never seen anything so funny before.

He started to laugh, too—but then, in the nick of time, he remembered that his name was Grouchy Bear. So he quickly turned the laugh into a cough before the others noticed he had actually laughed out loud.

Only Raggedy Ann saw what had happened, and she knew that Grouchy Bear was trying to hide his real feelings. But she didn't say a word.

The next day, Grouchy Bear went for a walk through the Deep Deep Woods.

"Tweet! Tweet!" He heard a small cry.

A baby sparrow was huddled on the path. Grouchy stopped and scooped up the tiny bird using his soft, furry paw.

"Are you lost, little bird?" he asked gently.

"No," she chirped. "I'm still learning how to fly. I flew out of the nest just right. But now I can't fly up again!" She flapped and fluttered her little wings.

"I'll help you," Grouchy Bear said. The little bird showed him where her nest was. Grouchy placed her on his shoulder and wrapped his paws around the tree trunk. Very carefully, he climbed up to the right branch. The baby bird hopped into her nest.

"Thanks!" chirped the baby's mother. "Are you new in the playroom?"

"Everyone will be there," barked Raggedy Dog.

"You must certainly come, Grouchy Bear," said Raggedy Ann. "This is a parade for bears! The bears from miles around will be there. There will be clown bears and marching bears and bears on floats and bears in bands!"

Grouchy Bear really wanted to go to the parade. But he wondered what his playroom friends would think if they saw him singing and marching and having fun. How could he be grouchy then?

"Humph," Grouchy Bear mumbled. "It sounds like a silly old parade."

And so the other dolls left him in the playroom and, with much excitement, set off on their way.

Grouchy Bear sat by himself. He heard his friends laughing as they trooped down the stairs. Grouchy Bear pouted. He tried to be grumpy. He tried to be grouchy. But he just didn't feel like it!

"I want to have fun!" he said to himself. And he ran right down the back stairs, through the door, and across the garden behind his friends.

The dolls were having such a good time that they didn't even notice Grouchy Bear quietly tagging behind them.

Only Raggedy Ann saw him. She was glad that Grouchy Bear decided to come along.

"We're almost there," Raggedy Ann called out as they made their way through the Deep Deep Woods.

And sure enough, in just a few steps, they came to a large clearing. Right in front of them was a brightly painted sign.

"Welcome to the Teddy Bear Parade!"

Grouchy Bear hid behind a big bush. Now that he was at the parade, he felt shy. What if everyone laughed at a grouchy bear who wanted to have a good time? Grouchy peeked out.

There were teddy bears everywhere he looked. Some climbed on trees. Others rolled on the grass. Each bear looked different, and all of them were having fun.

Grouchy Bear looked around.

"Oh!" he gasped. Under a tree not very far from him was the ballerina doll from the Town Toy Store!

Grouchy started toward his old friend. She knew him very well. He didn't have to be grouchy or shy around her. She might know what he should do. But just as he was about to wave . . .

a trumpet rang out loudly, *"Ta-ra! Ta-ra!"* Grouchy Bear turned around. There stood a very big teddy bear holding a trumpet and wearing a bright red jacket.

"I'm Theodore," the big bear said in a very important voice.

"Ooh!" said the ballerina doll.
"Aah!" said the playroom dolls.
Grouchy could tell he was a very important bear.
"The parade is about to begin," Theodore said. "Will all the teddy bears please line up?"

Grouchy Bear sat behind the bush. What should he do? Thinking that no one would notice, he let a tear roll down his furry cheek.

Another tear followed the first. Grouchy felt very sorry for himself. Suddenly someone was gently wiping the tears away with a soft handkerchief. It was Raggedy Ann!

"Why, Grouchy Bear! Aren't you going to march in the parade?" asked Raggedy Ann.

"Grouchy bears don't like to have fun," he explained.

"Are you sure that's always true?" Raggedy Ann asked.

Grouchy Bear realized at that very moment that what he said wasn't true at all. In fact, *he* was a grouchy bear, and he sure did want to have fun. Grouchy Bear didn't know what to say. "Ummmmm . . ." he started.

Raggedy Ann gave him a pat. "Just show how you feel," she said. "All the dolls and toys from the playroom would be proud to see you march. Why don't you join in?"

Grouchy Bear smiled a little smile. Then it got bigger.

Grouchy Bear hopped up. He smoothed his fur and stuck out his chest.

"Thanks, Raggedy Ann," he said. Then he quickly rushed over to join the line.

"Who will lead the parade?" Theodore called out to all the teddies. There was murmuring and chattering in the crowd. Suddenly a little teddy bear said, "That happy-looking bear looks just right for the job!" He pointed right at Grouchy.

"Me?" Grouchy asked in a whisper.

Theodore took Grouchy right to the front of the line.
"Look!" cried Sunny Bunny.
"It's Grouchy Bear!" said Bubbles the Clown Doll.
"He's having fun!" Raggedy Andy shouted.

Grouchy Bear beamed with pride. His heart was beating quickly and his knees were shaking.

Grouchy took one step forward. All the other bears took one step forward, too. Then he began to march. Everyone was marching right behind him!

The teddy bears marched for miles and miles as the
dolls and toys cheered them on. They splashed through
streams. They climbed up hills and rolled down again. They
sang and joked and laughed.

As they marched, Grouchy thought, "No one laughed at me! I guess I can be grouchy sometimes and happy sometimes. The mother sparrow and Raggedy Ann were right. It's how I feel inside that counts."

When the parade wound its way back to the clearing, Grouchy Bear was surrounded by his playroom friends. "What a surprise!" exclaimed Raggedy Andy. "We thought you only wanted to be a grumpy, grouchy bear!"

Grouchy Bear smiled a great big bear smile. "That was before I learned to show how I feel."

Raggedy Ann's eyes twinkled. She knew how Grouchy Bear was feeling.

He was feeling happy!

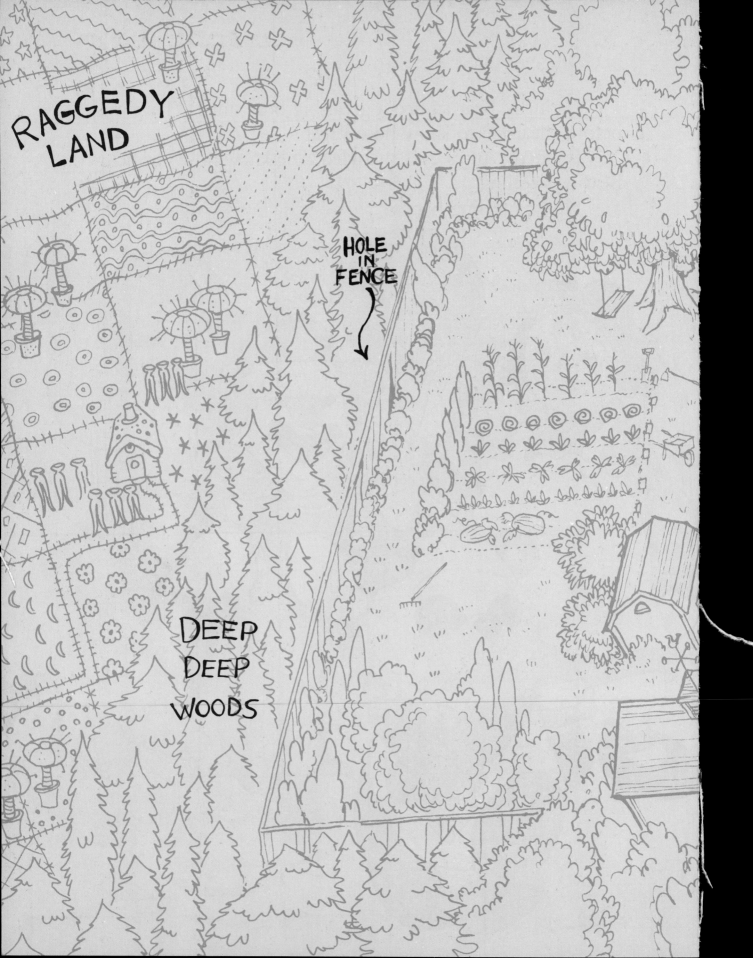